I0518886

Jackson's Love

An unfolding reflection . . .

Jackson's Love

An unfolding reflection . . .

Dana B. Lichtstrahl

Copyright © 2014 Dana B. Lichtstrahl

All rights reserved.
Printed in the United States of America.
First Edition

For information about permission to reproduce selections from this
book contact Dana B. Lichtstrahl at info@danalichtstrahl.com;
www.danalichtstrahl.com

Library of Congress Control Number: 2014913164

ISBN: 0977784452
ISBN-13: 978-0-9777844-5-5 (soft cover)

1. Dogs, Pets. 2. Fiction. 3. Inspiration. 4. Love.
5. Romance.

. . . Thank You,

Mom, without you
this story would not have been shared,

and

Dad, your keen editorial eye and "thumbs up"
added significantly to the excitement.

Contents

Dear Reader . . .

I offer a "Punctuation Disclaimer" for the use of all
those "?!" and "!?" throughout this book. Sometimes
questions happened first and at other times shock,
excitement, and/or exhilaration happened,
and questioning came soon after.

And those ellipsis and parentheses marks, (. . .),
they are all my, or someone else's, unfinished thoughts . .
.

And the translation of (lol) is, "laugh out loud".

Also, most of this story is fiction . . . I think.

1

Nirvana

Without too much consideration of a beginning, middle or end, I'll start with now, the only truly trustworthy moment. After all, who can actually say where the beginning, middle, or end of anything really is?! You think it's the end . . . yet it's not .

It's the beginning of May (2014) and I am at the end (I'm anticipating) of having "caught" the flu, about a week and one day back. No I did not have a flu shot. They make me sick. I can't recall the last time I was so physically uncomfortable. Which is why I'll share the "mattress story" first, since it fits right in with the flu. Especially since the last two nights I dragged my sorry ass to the living room couch and slept there. The couch is probably twenty five years old, yet still way better then the current king mattress, on the floor, on which I've been sleeping.

For over thirty years, I slept on the same mattress (I have nothing against new furniture). It was a sweet little Queen, foam, which sat on top of a Swedish-design platform bed. It was simple, and stunning, and oh so comfortable. It was my marital bed. I got it in the divorce. I loved it. Slept like joy on it. It was a place of the life and times of family; marriage, babies, then little boys, divorce, suitors after divorce, then two dogs, then take one dog away, you get the picture . . .

Then one year, about two years back, I put it on the floor, and its platform frame in the basement. I had wanted a sort of "artists bedroom", Bohemian in style and space. A bedroom in which I could bring large blank-framed canvases, and paint with acrylics anytime the spirit moved. The floor seemed like a novel place for the mattress. A year later the platform part was hauled away with most of the other stuff in the basement after a great rain storm had left half of its downpour down there, which is a different story . . . everything is so connected. (You can't *really tell a story* that doesn't have to do with anything else, right?) Then the mattress began to feel uncomfortable. Ugh!

So as I slept in my favorite Queen's lap on the floor, now without choice of rising up again, I started to ache. Not what I wanted. I tossed and turned and tossed and tossed and tossed and that was lousy. I hadn't known this kind of sleep, or rather no sleep. I knew sleep as eight, or nine hours nightly without a toss. I loved to sleep! So when Queenie, my mattress-of-experiences, my great sandbox of stories, began to feel uncomfortable, I got very sad. I knew I couldn't keep something that upon arising in the morning, caused my hips to radiate with pain in ways I had never dreamed.

A year passes. (I seem to be able to bear discomfort for long periods of time. I'm not really bragging.) It's June of last year, and my dear friend Lisa rents her furnished house to a new tenant. This one wants some of the furniture out. So I help by dragging my friend George into the process (we needed extra muscle and perspective). One of the first pieces to be moved was Lisa's trundle bed, a gorgeous chocolate-ty brown arched headboard, with two side boards (think couch), and it happened to be topped with the most glorious gold-colored pillows and comforter, with gold tassels and cord, fit for a princess with all that rich fabric . . . It came with two twin mattresses. One sat on the main frame and the other sat on a frame that tucked under the main frame (maybe that's the trundle part?). The bottom frame and mattress could be raised to be even with the main frame so you could sleep on it as if it were a king size bed. Lisa kept it in her office as a showpiece, (one bed tucked under the other), or if an occasional houseguest came, that's where they slept. In other words, it was practically brand new.

Lisa and George knew my old Queenie was hurtin' and "highly" recommended it be tossed and I take the trundle bed with all its trimmings. "Way too much energy stored in Queenie!" George stated emphatically. What the heck did he know! It was a sandbox of great experiences! Maybe if Lisa hadn't nodded in agreement with him, Queenie might have had a chance. Yet, I was a sleeper in need of a bed, and my eyes glazed over in delight at all that plush gold bedding, so I paid Lisa $200 for all of it, put it in my Jeep and drove it home.

Then George and I took my Queenie mattress out of my bedroom, down the stairs, then outside, and leaned her up against the house. I didn't much like that. It seemed so odd that Queenie was now under the open sky (unprotected) . . . And if she was leaning against the house, the next step was out the gate and into a garbage truck on some future Thursday morning. The house is a left half of a duplex. There is only one side. Once on the outside, you rarely got to come back in. Queenie was out there for about two weeks. When putting out the garbage I'd look at her, lean up against her and give her a hug. I'd find myself yearning for her back in my room. I don't think anyone saw me. It was as if Queenie was alive and I was tossing a life. I'd get all teary. I'd regret the new trundle. It was the strangest experience. It really is true, we *make* the experiences with our stuff, and then it becomes sacred because we've christened it so. It rained very hard for several days. The following Thursday morning I was determined to remove it from the premises. I could no longer watch as it slowly crumpled; the foam now like an enormous sponge monument and as heavy too. It needed to move on for my sanity. It wasn't in plastic (which is how a mattress needs to be wrapped these days for pick up), yet armed with a $20 bill for the garbage guys, and assuring them it was bug-less, I watched as they hauled Queenie through the gate, and into the back of the "waste vehicle", which then swallowed her. Watching her absorbed by a big green, steel-eating piece of machinery was gruesome. I had a lot of stories attached to Queenie! Exhale. Why did I listen to my *friends*!? Why am I disposing of her life?! (because of your hip pain . . . it's a mattress . . . oh yeah.)

Over thirty year old mattress out, new twins in.

George and I schlepped the trundle with all its parts, upstairs and set it up so the bed was in king size position. Wow. A king was so big! There was so much space up there. This is so ridiculous I can hardly explain my sleeping-events that unfolded from there. I'll try to make it brief and interesting—it was so very laughable, (on and off of course).

The two twin mattresses ran horizontal on the trundle. When you sleep the length of the bed, your head is toward one sideboard and your feet are at the other. You are sleeping with your body parallel with the headboard (or backboard). Got it (you're surrounded on three sides)? Later, when the trundle was set up with the twins running horizontal in their respective frames, my Mom and I (yet another story) dashed out to Walmart and bought two king foam bed-pads to throw on top and make things even more comfy, (Lisa's twins were not top grade, yet the "bedding" was over the top). Also, I wanted to sleep with my *head* at the headboard (and not my back, which I did for a while and which didn't work for me). I wanted the full king experience, properly.

Ok, so I slept across the twins, or rather perpendicular, and there I sort of stayed . . . even though only *one* of my dogs could jump up on to it, it was so very unexpectedly high—certainly a truly big difference from having Queenie directly on the floor. It had not even crossed my mind that I would no longer be sleeping with *both* my dogs, once the trundle was erected.

Sometimes I'd sit and stare at the whole king-contraption from across the bedroom in my writing chair. It was a regal set-up. It just wasn't comfortable. I could feel the hard steel where the two bed frames were supposed to have been level, even through the four inches of fairly sturdy foam Mom and I had topped it with (imagine The Princess and the Pea) . . . and only one dog could jump to its plateau! *What was that*?! Nikki, my Australian Cattle dog mix could. She had longer legs and more "spring" in them. Jackson my

Border Collie mix could not . . . and then I was kind of liking a little less hair all around (which came mostly from Nikki . . . Geez life is so unpredictable.)

Here is where my stories have a difficult time separating. I should probably introduce the whole Jackson aspect here, yet I'm trying to provide enough background while getting you to the part where we meet at a café, yes, that's right . . . So I'll stay with the mattress story until that's done, (giving a glimpse of the Jackson story), because the café part will blow you away—(it did me).

With my sons telling me how odd the bed looked from the previous one and without sleeping with either of my dogs, (if one couldn't get up, the other wasn't coming), there was lots of unused space up there (Nikki and Jackson always slept together back to back). Six months later in a fiery emission of energy motivated by back pain frustration, (it must have been 2:00 a.m.), I swung up out of bed and proceed to quickly slide both twins the wrong way on their frames. I did this thinking I wouldn't feel the hard edge where the bed frames were supposed to meet and be *level*. Unfortunately, with the twins running perpendicular to their frames, like me, the hard edge where the frames met caused a slight rise in both mattresses directly across my hip-zone and, because the trundle's frames are wire, the twins sagged everywhere else. This is nuts, right!? You may be wondering why I did not simply go out and buy a decent bed and call it a night (or a good night's sleep), which leads to another story, tightly wound around the others . . .

So, I tossed and turned and tossed and tossed and tossed, it was lousy. I tossed right into October 2013. And on October 22nd, while working at the dining room table one afternoon with Jackson curled at my feet and Nikki curled in a living room chair, Jackson had a seizure—of a grand sort. He was eight. When he was gently laid on the steel table for the Veterinarian's review, over forty minutes later, he was still in seizure, a long time to be shaking uncontrollably, foaming at the mouth, urinating, and pooping simultaneously. He had worked up a fever of 107°. Immediately he was induced to relax, with his paw hooked to an intravenous feed . . . He died that evening around 10:15 p.m. Details to come . . . but not too much.

I slept the 2013 holidays away on that crazy trundle and on into the New Year, (Nikki now came up on the bed frequently and I wanted it that way, hair and all). I tossed and turned and tossed and tossed and tossed.

Which brings us back to now (May 2014), with the flu and feeling exceptionally depleted, Nikki and I were working at the dining room table, her at my feet, (it was highly unusual for her to hang near me as Jackson had, 24/7). She rose quickly to announce that someone was at the front door, which was open with the screen door locked. Barely a breeze entered. It was hot. It was George. First words out of his mouth were, "I got something that will *change your life forever! Follow me!*" I followed him out the front door, down the porch steps and out into the street where a king mattress wrapped in plastic, straddled a wagon hooked to an SUV. What can I say!? Generous beyond belief, yes, yet the sinking feeling in my stomach wasn't connecting to "generosity". It was already at, "*Nope! This is not the mattress for me!*" I had eyed it on the wagon and knew right away it was a softy. Ugh! The trundle being wire-strung already sagged and imagining "Mr. Softie" on top . . . well . . . "*Ok, what the heck! It's going to be great . . . anything is better than the twins!*" I noticed crossing my mind.

Two twins out, new king in. (Those twins were thrown off that trundle so fast and leaned up against the dinning room wall, *versus the side of the house*, and that king was flung right on top of the whole unleveled-metal-and-wire-strung-trundle-bed mess.)

It was the biggest, heaviest mattress I had ever met. It was a *King*. I think that was on a Saturday. The following Monday I woke up with such lower back pain I could hardly get up and off the damn thing, which is why I was glad it was high off the floor. Swinging my legs over the edge and then planting my feet on the ground was beyond helpful. My life seemed like an episode right out of *Curb Your Enthusiasm*. I had the flu. I was a mess. I got right on the phone to Sophia. She knew both George and me, and could offer some good, clear, mattress guidance. I tried. I really tried. Maybe it was the flu, or maybe just because it was a softy, I could not get a good nights sleep on Kingy! Really! And where the bed frames met, the mattress buckled right across my hip-zone. Go figure. It had now been two years of (Princess and the Pea) "Sleepless in Jersey"! The whole thing began to stink like the 1993, irritatingly funny movie, Ground Hog Day. Over and over and . . .

It was 7:00 a.m. Monday, and I was crying hysterically as I phoned Sophia in Florida. She picked up and I could hear her sanity through my hysteria. "*I can't sleep on this king mattress any more . . . sob, sob . . . How can someone buy a mattress for someone else as a surprise!? . . . sob . . . a mattress is a very personal thing . . . sob, sob! Heck, I like firm, not soft!*" Sophia listened like the master healer she is and then said, "Tell him he needs to take it back." I was truly comforted. We hung up and then George called saying, "*I am so sorry! We will get you the right mattress, yadayadayada . . .*" Ridiculous right?

A week later with both of us still schlepping around the flu, (did I mention I had caught it from him when he spent a week on my living room couch . . . different story . . .), sweating, exhausted, George and I deconstructed

the trundle (on the first 80 degree day in May, which was
a bit of a hindrance), and put the king on the floor to
make some correction to King Softy (until its
replacement arrived). We took the trundle parts to the
basement. It was the end of an era. I was back on the
floor with my mattress, this time a king. We hoped for
the best. It was now certainly more doggie-accessible.
I pictured Jackson laying at the foot back to back with
Nikki . . . maybe the floor would be the solution . . .

It took one night to know the floor was not going to
make this King any firmer. A new mattress must be
picked out . . . The very next day in the pouring rain,
George picked me up at Noon. We had to be back by
3:00 p.m. and it was almost an hour west, one-way, to the
mattress warehouse, (King Softie's origin). We were on a
mission and it was going to be a quick one. I got into his
car carrying a bowl filled with a hotdog on a bun, chips
and tomatoes (it was all I could muster). "Here" I said,
"here's lunch." We were both hanging on by a thread (of
humor). We felt a little better than shit. It seemed like
the flu would live on into eternity through both of us.
Once at Vince's, George's high school friend who owned
the mattress warehouse, I threw my weary body across
each plastic covered mattress he advised me to test (the
plastic alone is enough to throw off your mattress-sense) .
. . until, I reached Nirvana! There I stopped. "You like
that one!?" he said with a sneaky smile. "That's a highly

unusual mattress! It's a *memory foam*." Foam? Did
someone say *foam*?! I love foam! . . . and Nirvana was a
Queen not a king, and Vince said once on box springs
she would feel even more remarkable, (I had humanized
her already). He wrote my name on its plastic cover in
black marker. Then I awaited her arrival. Between the
mattress, the floor and the flu, I couldn't recall a more
uncomfortable time, (did I already mention that?!)

A potential foreclosure pending was not easing any of
the pain. It had been a rough four years of earning little
to none, which had its moments of deep depression, and
(strangely enough) heights of contentment too. Needless
to say, it had been a rather out-of- the-ordinary time.
I lived in Jersey, which also seemed to be the foreclosure
capital of the nation. I had so little understanding of how
my life had become so uncomfortable in so many ways.
I thought I had talent and skill that could be exchanged
on the open market. Ok . . . I get that the whole economy
tanked. Yet still, it seemed every door I had knocked on,
remained closed; proposal after proposal, job prospect
after prospect, in-person interview, or otherwise, nothing
had opened. The Red Sea had not parted, the Promised
Land was locked tight. Yet, with my new hand picked
mattress, I felt somewhat like Goldilocks who had found
something just right, even with the possibility of owning
such an extraordinary queen foam mattress, with no roof
to put it under.

Nirvana was on the way . . .

2

Jackson

Just a little background, we don't need to go deeply into everything (too much detail can cause indigestion). Jackson's death was not just uncomfortable, it was beyond that. It blew apart my world. He was my glue and my bedrock over the last eight years (while the boys were growing up). Big pause (no pun). And I determined whether he stayed or left, in the end.

Laid on the steel table for the Vet's review—carried in from the back of my Jeep—Jackson was still shaking, foaming, shitting; all my prayers and focused love hadn't adjusted any of that. I felt helpless, weak in the knees. His paw was hooked to an intravenous drip system flowing liquid anesthesia, (if I recall correctly). This would relax him, unknotting his muscles, allowing his temperature to cool. He was hot. He stopped thrashing. I hovered over him as staff prepared to move him to a ground-floor cage. One I could crawl into with him, practically. His eyes had closed and he seemed peacefully sleeping. I was told he would wake up around 6:00 p.m. and to come back then and, "we would understand more". During the past year, Jackson had had two other semi-brain happenings. One with something called Horner's Syndrome, a kind of Bell's palsy in dogs, and the other, Lyme disease; neither pleasant. At one point his face (skin and muscles) had drooped so, it prevented him from seeing well from both eyes. He (miraculously) returned to new within weeks. Maybe if I hadn't had him shaved six months earlier as the groomer recommended. Maybe if I hadn't done that, (because later I find out from George, *"Never* shave Border Collies.") Maybe that weakened him, maybe if I had been more informed . . .

I returned to the vet-hospital at 5:00 p.m. (prepared to drive Jackson home) and walked down the hall and crawled directly into his cage (as much of me would fit). He was still sleeping. I began to sing to him quietly, his eyes closed, *"I love you, a bushel and a peck . . . "* (I think Mom taught me that song long ago, I don't know why it surfaced then). I wondered if he knew I was there. At 6:00 p.m. the Vet came by and seemed a little concerned. "He should have started to come awake by now." He murmured looking at me. I didn't much like that. He checked his "vitals" and left. 7:00 p.m., 8:00 p.m. and 9:00 p.m. passed. Jackson was still sleeping deeply. How deep, I had no knowledge. 9:30 p.m. and the Vet, after having occasionally checked-in, came over extremely concerned. Jackson hadn't shown any difference in his state since he was "relaxed". The hospital was closing for the night at 10:00 p.m. I could leave him and he might wake up—in what shape wasn't known. I could take him home and he could wake up there back to normal, or in a seizure, picking up where it had left off. Then again, he may not wake up anywhere. The Vet said this would happen again.

Jackson was a pup in a batch that was sent north from Mississippi after storm Katrina in 2005. He came with his brother. They had been labeled, "Bert and Ernie". By Noon, after my youngest son Tim had completed his SSAT exams for possible, private, middle-school admission, we went to adopt him. I had found him online through a dog-rescue organization. The flea market that had set up a holding kennel on their grounds was about to close that Saturday, and we were lost driving in a maze of country roads trying to beat the clock. Our call to them helped steer us there before closing. Tim saw him first and pointed, "There, Mom!" The volunteer went up to a cage with one dog in it. Bert had been adopted in the early morning (by someone who knew how to get there), it was now 3:00 p.m. She held out Ernie. Tim's eyes opened wide and a smile drew across his face. He sat down on the concrete floor with the pup. Ernie was about four months old. It was

January 2006, and that pup melted away every lousy frozen trauma you ever had, when looking into his eyes. Even at four months, he had the eye contact of a Buddha. When you gazed into Ernie's eyes, there was the experience of gazing into deep, dark pools of the infinite, so warm and welcoming. They were big and brown, outlined in black like some Egyptian prince reincarnate. And those eye lashes! Women would die for those, I thought. Golden facial fur to an all black long haired coat (which would grow even longer over time). He was stunning. Smart. So very smart. I wrote the check for $350, to cover his medical costs, signed a few papers, Tim scooped him up and we left, allowing the volunteers to finally close their cages for the night.

In the back seat on the way home, Tim placed a blanket across his lap and Ernie climbed on top naturally. I had no idea then, how much this new addition to our family would shift my life forever. The story was just unfolding. I was a single Mom with two sons (Kyle was four years older than Tim), and now a dog.

Did I even know how to care for one!?

Once home, I thought of him as "love walking", and whenever he walked inside, his long nails tap-danced on the wood floors throughout the house (because I didn't believe in clipping them, actually I was too afraid I'd cut them too short, and hurt him). That tap-dancing was music to my ears. When you watched that little bundle of legs and fur, and heard that tap-tapping across the floor, you received a sense of Heaven on Earth.

First there was the name change to "Jackson", which was Tim's choice. Kyle and I went with it. Done. Next there was "house training", translation: peeing and pooing outside versus inside. When I found myself on the kitchen floor three months later crying, upset and believing I was going to screw up this little dog's life (now seven months old and not so well trained in the bathroom-arts), Jackson came over to me and looked directly into my eyes. That was all that was needed to dissolve my worry. His direct look was dazzling. There was a fundamental warmth there that grounded me every time as if to say, "*You are love, you can't go wrong*".

10:15 p.m. on October 22, 2013, I signed the paper for Jackson to be set free from his body, the cage within the cage. What more can I say? I drove home alone, empty. I was completely broken by that, then.

We had Jackson for four years before Nikki came to our side gate one day in October 2009, (Octobers seemed to be a very "doggie" month). I swear she came as if she knew Jackson lived there. I was having an open-house-yard-sale, Tim was out and Kyle was completing his last year at his university. There was lots of activity, and the guy I was dating at the time was assisting. I let her through the gate to check her tags for a contact number. From the moment she entered the garden, Jackson loved her. She had a ruddy auburn face, long white legs and coat, with ears like a Wolverine. (What's not to love?) I called the number on one of her dangling dog-tags and the organization that answered immediately connected me to her owner. He lived just at the top of the street. We had never met in the ten years I had lived there! That was a little unusual . . . It seemed his dog had left his yard by way of his mistakenly open gate. He said he would come right over. We hung up.

I never imagined a strikingly handsome thirty-something man to show up, claim his dog and introduce himself as "George". Yes, that's how we met. I didn't know he was a neighbor 'til Nikki came to the gate! Nikki and Jackson had many play dates and a year or so later, George had business in Florida and shared that he couldn't take her. I wasn't going to let her be returned to the rescue from which she came, which was George's Plan B, if another friend, (Plan A) didn't want her. So she moved in with us. We had Jackson for four years, then Nikki and Jackson together for another four, and then, in a moment, it was life with Nikki and Jackson was free of his doggie-body. Tim was living and working from home with me, and Kyle was in New York, exploring the world of music, people and cameras. The king mattress was on the floor and I was happily expecting Nirvana (on box springs).

This is where craziness escalates . . .

Seven months after Jackson left his body . . . a few days ago to be exact, I got my sorry ass out of bed (again, along with whatever flu was still clinging for its life), got dressed, put make-up on for the first time in two weeks, and walked out into the world and then into one of our neighborhood's local cafés. I was missing Jackson terribly. The plan was to sit there with a cup of black coffee and regroup, (reassess the passing of my pup, my sickness, my income, my home, imagine Nirvana, yadayadayada . . .). It was just after 3:00 p.m., unusually late for me to be drinking. I suppose I needed a reboot while regrouping. I was also experiencing serious cabin fever even though I wasn't really sure if my home was going to continue to be my cabin. Sitting with my head buried in my journal, coffee (no more tea please) in hand, and imagining the delivery of my new bed, I sensed someone there, hovering. Maybe it was someone in line . . . I slowly looked up and found myself staring into big brown eyes framed in remarkable lashes, seeming weirdly too familiar. I was a tad sick and a little caffeinated. I was looking at a man and he was looking at me. There was something inspiring about him. *That right there was unusual.* I hadn't connected to an energetically-inspiring man since my divorce fifteen years back. Kids had come, (one had left the nest), as had a dog, and a suitor or three, (none of which I found exciting enough to have stay . . . I was no longer dating the previous guy, it was an agreed-on goodbye). I was smiling now.

With our eyes engaged, out of the mouth of this most exceptionally handsome man fell the words, "*Hello, I'm Jackson*". Tears instantaneously welled-up burning my eye-sockets just hearing his name. What reality *was* I experiencing!? I'm sure my jaw dropped just enough to look completely Gob-smacked. OMG! WHAT THE HECK!? WHAT'S HAPPENING HERE?! "Can we talk?" he then says. I think silently . . . *can we talk?* Who is this guy?! Who *am I?!*

Without me responding, he sat on a chair that he grabbed from another table and set near me and began to introduce himself further, "I relocated here from Mississippi in 2005." *Noooooo!* This can't be happening . . . this isn't happening! Someone put acid in my coffee and I'm hallucinating big-time! It's the flu! I'm *really* sick! My mind was flipping through its knowledge to make some sort of reasonable connection for understanding the situation! My left hand was now involuntarily covering my mouth. I quickly removed it as if to feel more confident and welcoming of the whole bizarre situation. There were people in the café. I didn't want attention. I stared at the large brown eyes and those long lashes. I felt their kind warmth. I took a breath and continued with gentler focus, seeking some kind of clarity. My head was sort of spinning, and so I asked in a rather child-like way, "Are you my dog!?" (*What the "F"!? . . . couldn't I have said that waaay differently?! But that was what I meant! . . . My "selves" were engaged in opinion, as usual, and I was listening!*)

"Yes, I am" he replied matter-of-factly, and the way he batted those lashes just about made me weep with excitement. Oh My God, OMG! (I was saying and writing that frequently then.) COULD THIS GUY BE MY DOG INCARNATE?! OK people, what would *you* do if your beloved animal of the opposite sex came back as an exceptionally handsome man, or woman and found you!? *Would that be good?!*

"Well . . . just . . . what *are* you thinking . . . Jackson?!" I blurted out terribly unstably. "I'm thinking maybe you and Nikki and Tim should move in with me." (*Whaaaat?! How did he know their names?!*) "Didn't we just meet?" My reply was crusty. "Well, actually", he responded calmly and warmly, "We've known each other for eight and a half years and have already lived together—differently—yet together. Somehow, in this body I know you and your little family . . . " His manor was that of someone right out of the 1940's. A Cary Grant-ish type, he was dressed in a classic dark suit as if having come from work. Nice threads. Nice shoes too. He had great style. I loved his tie, artful. And his voice, oh my, oh my. I could listen to that for a very long time— uninterrupted. So I couldn't disagree with his answer, it seemed reasonable, especially because of the way he made it sound. If he *really was Jackson-dog*, which he said he was, didn't I *want* to be with him?! (Thinking happened . . . *where was he going to sleep!? . . . at the foot of my new bed?! . . . and my home wasn't yet financially stable! . . . HIS home?* (a mind can wander). . . *and this isn't a good time for a relationship! (Somebody smack me! . . . this was my dog I was listening to . . . ?!)*

Right then and there my mind scanned who I could call for a reality check. Sophia? George? This was too crazy for *everyone. Maybe we could date. Date my dog?! Why isn't he having any difficulty with this? I suppose I don't have to tell anyone. His name could be a simple coincidence. I could just work through this on my own, I'm just hanging out with a guy I met at a coffee shop . . . yadayadayada . . .* (I was aware of speed thinking).

"Jackson," I said, "do you understand me?" (I couldn't believe I said *that!*) His eyes rolled, (what did I expect, *I didn't even know what I meant*)! What a dumb question!

24

I had acted as if he had just learned English! (Had he?!)
He must have been around my age—in his 40"s . . . *didn't
I still have his ashes in the gold can on my shelf? Didn't I
have his whole body?!* Jackson's new body definitely
looked alive and well, about six feet, two inches of sturdy
flesh and bones, from where I was sitting. He began to
smile and then he looked directly into my eyes, like a
Buddha. That redirected my piling-up fearful thoughts,
and that this was the theatre of the absurd. Then I asked
softly, and a bit reluctantly "Do you dance?" *What was I
thinking!?* "Of course I dance," he replied. I was right
then, truly out of my league. This tall, dark brown-eyed
man with those lashes can shake his booty!? Did I make
this up?! Is this the Law of Attraction at its best?! Why
can't I do this with money?! *Doesn't matter!*

"Let's do that Friday night." He suggested quite
naturally. It was Tuesday. "Here's my card," he offered.
"I'll pick you up at 9:30 p.m. Do you think you'll feel
better by then?" "Oh yes, *yes* I'm sure I will . . . *I'm
certain!*" I said way too quickly for confidence. Then he
gathered his stuff and left. WOW. I took a deep breath
and released it while looking around. That stabilized me.
I closed my journal which had been open on my lap the
whole time—his business card now inside, I stood up
slowly collecting myself, walked over to the trash bucket
threw in my cup, and hobbled home. Tim was at work.
He would definitely get what happened (he's a brilliant,

open-source-thinking 19 year old). Maybe I'd see him tomorrow, yet our moments of connection had been like ships at dusk passing, with seconds of exchanging "Hello".

Once home, I changed into yoga pants and a t-shirt and crawled into bed explaining what had occurred to Nikki. She listened intently completely absorbed.

3

10:00 p.m.

On Thursday morning, (after encountering Jackson-man on Tuesday), Nirvana came. Vince and George (yes, still dear friends even after the King Softy disaster), appeared at my door ready to rearrange the whole mattress saga yet again. It had been almost two years since Queenie had lost her muscle and was consumed by the "waste vehicle", and a year since the trundle had been brought over, set up, taken down, etc.

In an intense instant of shoving King Softy back down through the old narrow staircase which it almost hadn't gone up, and sweating once again over a bed; King was out and Nirvana was in, on split box springs! Boy did she look just right. She even had a pattern on her like a swirling galaxy, which George remarked, reminded him of me!

"It's a foam, it's a foam – it's memory foam! Yaaaaay!" I cheered. "Yup, that right there is a *$2,500 memory foam mattress!*" Vince barked with excitement (He had

charged me pennies). Now *there* was a man who loved beds and knew all about them! "It will keep its memory for at least ten years." He shared. Hmmm, what then? I thought. Would it no longer remember me? Is that mattress-Alzheimer's? All right, ten years, that's plenty of good sleep! That will take me into my 50's . . . (I was dreaming of being Rip Van Winkle and sleeping for the next ten years, at least. I had catching up to do). I was definitely down with ten years of solid, nightly sleep. The deed was done. Nirvana was in place and I was back on the floor (or really on box springs), on a queen foam mattress—21st century foam! Is *that* Karma?! King Softy was on the wagon and Vince had tied the twins, which I offered to him free just to haul away, onto the roof of his SUV. He knew he could do something with them. They were practically brand new!

George brought in hoagies from the local shop and the three of us sat at my kitchen counter eating, in celebration of our recent accomplishment done ever so well, (even with two of us experiencing the last wee bit of the-clinging-alien-flu). Then they left for the south turnpike happy men, a full wagon trailing behind.

Sleeping on a king size mattress on the floor for just a little while and then sleeping on a queen size, it felt like my horizon had shrunk. It was a little awkward at first. Funny how quickly we can get used to something. Yet that night I came to realize Nirvana was a perfect size and, a very sexual bed, or perhaps sensual is a better word. She could wrap herself around parts of my body I had no idea I had. I tried to rock her . . . BOY was she sturdy, and steady! (No wire frame trembling, squeaking, shaking.) She didn't bounce, or sag! Maybe I should refer to her as genderless. Maybe it's best not to get too close. I understand Nirvana translates to "freedom"—double wow.

The next morning I sent George a text, "I have the best fucking bed." I imagined him forwarding it to Vince, or sharing it verbally. Joy to the world! Finally, after Queenie had stopped working properly two years back (hey, her memory lasted for thirty plus years), I woke up without pain, hip or otherwise, in just one 9-hour night of continuous, blissful, nurturing sleep. No tossing and tossing and turning, no, none of that! (Yes, it is possible.) Just one night of Nirvana and I was a happy sleeper once again. It was also Friday and Jackson-the-man was due to come by for me at 9:30 p.m. He knew where we lived. I never said, yet of course he knew! Maybe he wouldn't show up and then I could validate the hallucination of the whole Tuesday café-experience, which would feel a whole lot simpler than deciding what to wear when going out dancing with my former dog, now a classically-handsome man. (What would the neighbor's think?) Nikki would meet him in a few hours. Would she know something about "this Jackson" and then share it? I was counting on it.

Friday moved fast. I seemed to have an enormous amount of energy. I forgot that's what happens with an awesome night of deep sleep! Hadn't had one in years! By 4:30 p.m. I was feeding Nikki. By 7:30 p.m. I was in the tub. Give me hot water in which to soak, and the best ideas start popping (this happens when driving too). Yes, I take my journal both places and jot down the interesting stuff such as, "*If we went for a walk in the woods, would Jackson-man pee, go in the water and shake himself off, and then sniff the wildflowers?*"Well, that seemed reasonable even for a human . . . *What's the problem with that?!* Why had I kept imagining Jackson-man doing something very Jackson-dog-like, like licking himself somewhere . . . or barking, or something. It was as if I was preparing myself for such peculiar possibilities! I was having those expectations and experiencing them in nanoseconds without really *having* experienced them, (if you know what I mean). Since that was not the experience I wanted in a nanosecond, or otherwise, it was time to leave the tub.

It was exactly 9:30 p.m. She didn't bark. Oh geez, that right there was a "communication". Why didn't She bark? She *knew* him!? He had arrived on time wearing black pants, a dark-storm-blue shirt tucked in, topped with a thin black leather coat, with a waist-tie. It was a cool-ish May night (versus an 80 degree May day). He looked comfortable and dashingly good through the screen door. What a sight for feminine eyes! OK, I was wearing a somewhat clingy dress, patterned with teeny tiny, black and white polka dots, with three-quarter close-fitting sleeves, and the hem just touching the top of my knee. It had a moderately low v-neck. It was comfortable and sexy and I could dance wild in it (if so inspired). Nikki actually decided. My classic black pumps gave my five foot, six inch frame a bit more height. Dancing was a great idea!

I smiled a tentative smile, which I hadn't anticipated, and greeted him a little coolly. I wish I had been warmer in my welcome, however processing and arriving at a place other than, "This is my dog!?" hadn't yet happened (I was wishing it had). "Hi, come in," I invited. Nikki stepped back and gave him room to come through the screen door. "Hello", he said in that milky, pitch-perfect-for-my-ear voice, and walked right over to my big green couch and sat in the same spot Jackson-dog used to sit. Nikki had watched him. Hmmm . . . why did he pick that side? Ok. No worries. Then he offered his hand toward Nikki for sniffing. Nikki walked right over. (Nikki is skeptical of most male people of any age.) When she realized she knew him (or who he was maybe?), her energy suddenly changed and she pounced her two front paws right up

onto his knees as if to say, "*Where the heck ya been fella!?*
I know you!" Then she went happy-crazy! She backed off
his knees with such excited-force she almost lost her
balance. She raced up and down the stairs, and ran back
and forth between rooms, living room to dining room to
kitchen and back. She barked her happy playful bark,
and circled a few times near the couch where Jackson
(man or dog, whatever), sat. I stood there stunned. I had
counted on her to share her thoughts about this guy, and
wow had she come through. She was clearly saying she
knew this guy-dog-man-incarnate! (Jackson-the-dog used
to hump her at these playful times . . . *did I need to be*
concerned with that now?! . . . how did life get so
foreign?)

"I can assure you I am completely man, with no desire for
animals." he said head turning to the right to face me.
Damn! Could he read my mind, (as it seemed Jackson-
dog did at times), or was that common sense,
reasonable, for him to share at that moment?!

It was now 10:00 p.m. 30-minutes of "study" had
happened between all three of us, and it was time for him
to show me his "dance moves". (Ever since I was young I
loved to shake my booty to the rhythm of percussion. It
brought on joy instantly. So I was very much wanting to
experience my intimate joy of music, and this man.) Ok,
maybe I wasn't certain (oh *that* was just perfect). It was a

kind of, "*Maybe I don't want to do this . . . what if it's fun?*" Mixed with, "Is *that* why this is becoming so intensely uncomfortable?" I was scared I might *like him*?! I ignored my internal chatter, left a note for Tim, "Gone Dancing!", and out the door we went, leaving Nikki who had curled up on the big leather chair with a sense about her that the world was good.

Jackson owned a rather large black SUV. What did I imagine a six foot, two inch man to drive, a Mazda MX-5 Miata? (I don't really like those anyway, so close to the ground my butt is always clinched while on the road in them. Way too tight an experience for me! I prefer bigger, and up high, if given a choice.) The sound system was superior. He played the trumpet and piano and drums (I learned). Sound was important to him. He put on Santana circa 1970's. Perfect. The rhythm soothed me, which eased my potentially negative string of thoughts. I found myself seat-dancing just a bit. He smiled. The best club was 40 minutes east, so we had lots of time to chat it up and get to know each other better, (as man and woman?).

"I think Nikki likes me," he said, turning to look at me for a moment. "She does", I replied and continued, "Do you think she senses the Jackson-dog aspect about you?", I shared, still a tad defensive (it was obvious she had). I didn't have an effectively good grasp of *who* I was with. No rather, I didn't have an effectively good grasp of

myself! "You don't really have a beneficial understanding
of who I am," he reported and then asked, "do you?" "No"
I frowned feeling seen through, and so appealed, "I could
use some education." "Ok," he replied and continued,
"Just consider that the body and mind is a collection of
information and the power source that runs it, is a kind
of love-energy." "All right, I get that" (sort of, I think . . .
kind of), I said and countered, "So are you saying you are
Jackson-dog in a new body because the "love-energy" has
moved? Are we *really* talking reincarnation?" "Well," he
smiled, "A while back I seemed to have 'received', in this
form, a good amount of your 'Jackson-dog's experience',
which is why I was drawn to connecting with you. *And,*
I have other experiences too, 40-plus years of additional
information, which drew me to you as well, and all of it
blends . . . " Well that was rather rationally expressed
(sort of, kind of . . .), We were out of town and on the
highway already. He paused, lowered the sound of
Santana, and continued. "I think you see, or understand
me as your dog." I interrupted, "Well didn't you *say that's
who you were* at the café and aren't you saying that now?"
(Why was I having conflict with this perfectly adorable
being!? And, he was so not defensive!) He caught my
eyes for a short second and I fell into warmth. That kind
of warmth stops me every time and I hadn't recalled
feeling this with a man . . . only a male dog! "Yes, yet if
you can imagine Jackson-dog's personality, his spirit, or
maybe you might say his soul and aspects of his

intelligence—although he's certainly smarter and I'm maybe, more aware . . . " I was all ears, listening intently. "Dogs have enormous capabilities to sense, communicate and experience life, as do humans . . . you might think of me as *enhanced* with Jackson-dog's qualities, rather than simply 'dog-turned-man' . . . as if his *qualities* sort of 'blew into me' and I became aware of them, and yet I'm also Jackson the man who has lived over forty years, etc." Still smiling and calm, feeling much more at ease, I couldn't wait to dance, and I was aware that if my story could shift ever so slightly, (which I think it was in the process of doing), and I could understand this "meeting" ever so positively, we could be having the time of our life—now!

The club was a sprawling place. One DJ, two dance floors, three or four bars, bathrooms in all corners, tables, booths, food, celebration, you get the picture. Oh yes and a light show in synch with the music! Making our way, he walked slightly ahead of me maneuvering us through the crowd, his right hand halfway around my waist guiding me. He eyed a spot on the main dance floor and took us there. We danced. Yes, yes, yes! He knew rhythm and was comfortable, no rather he was intimate with his body! How cool was that! He had "moves like Jagger", and as the song, "Soul Sister" by Train shouts, "*The way you move ain't fair you know!*" was a perfect description of him from my perspective! He also knew how to dance together! Turning me, stepping back and forth together, we were a wave of movement hour after hour! I was dripping. (Which is one reason I love to dance. It's such a cardio-workout!) By 1:00 a.m. we were downing bottled water at the bar to revitalize. By 1:30 a.m. we decided we were pleasantly "cooked" and all shook out. We drove home talking about other lives, and galaxies and questioned extraterrestrials . . .

I wanted to know where he grew up, did he have brothers, sisters, did he read, prefer movies, what was his favorite food, what politicians did he back, and where did he go to find peace; beaches, mountains, the tub? We hadn't gotten to much of that when we arrived back at my place. We parked, he got out, opened my car door and walked with me toward the house. The porch light was off and the streetlight a few feet away lit the front steps only. We walked up the steps onto the porch and stood there laughing at life and its unusual components such as humans and dogs, and time travel . . . BOY was he sexy there, in that half-lit moment. Tingling with excitement was a good thing. It meant I was still very much alive, and, it was time to say "Good Night". No, I wasn't going to invite him in. Maybe he sensed that. "Gimmie a kiss," I did say jokingly like I used to say to J-dog (and I wondered if he knew *that*). He moved in closer and touched his nose to mine (that's what J-dog would have done). That close to him, and my happy-meter just about exploded and then, he licked my lips—just like Jackson-dog did! So surprised I burst out laughing! He smiled, held my glance and said in his smoothest silkiest laugh, "KIDDING!", turned and left. He rolled down his car window as he rolled off and blew a kiss. Nikki caught it as I opened the door and she listened as I changed out of my polka dots and into my yoga pants and t-shirt. We climbed into Nirvana and melted away into her memory . . .

4

txt

I wanted to stay in Nirvana forever. She was dream-like,
truly. It was morning and I lay there weightless on her
ocean of foam. She remembered every nook and cranny
of my form like she was water and I the rocks, filling
herself in here and there. Nirvana was very much like old
Queenie was in her early years. The thought crossed my
mind, "Would I sleep in Nirvana for the full ten years, or
more, or would she be given to Tim and I sleep in
someone else's Nirvana?" (It was obvious I was
entertaining thoughts of Jackson-man) All the ways
seemed more open, ready, possible. (Was that what
happens with a solid night of deep, refreshing sleep, or
Karma, or the Law of Attraction, or . . . ?!) I wasn't sure
about the stability of the roof over our heads, yet here I
was daydreaming about all good things. As long as a
positive idea appeared, there was more joy of course, and
that was seriously wanting to happen with me in regards
to Jackson-man, or rather my perspective of the whole
experience was wanting such an overhaul. What had

been there, my rigid perspective, wasn't working for me as well as I knew it could.

Once out of Nirvana, I told Nikki over breakfast that my head was filled with the agitation of my rigid preconceived notions of this "J-guy situation". The good, the bad and the ugly, were getting sticky. Already 10:00 a.m. Saturday, and it was time to call Mom and see if she wanted to go shoe shopping (we never buy retail, and we always use coupons, or we may not buy. It's more of a shoe game, then shoe shopping.) I think I just needed good company and some distraction while I processed a week of thoughts!

I am forty six, which makes Mom, well, older, yet once I arrived at her door, she still preferred driving us around. Was I going to bring up Jackson, man, or dog? I didn't even recall telling her that George had arranged a new mattress for me. With the flu and all, I hadn't seen her except for the day she drove me to the emergency room to confirm whether, or not, my flu had morphed into walking-pneumonia (I was just a week into the flu, then). Of course it hadn't. With lungs clear she drove me home while expressing that I ought to have taken the doctor's card in case I wanted to call him, (which really had more to do with "a relationship" and less about health . . . she is such a matchmaker at heart and I do think she and Dad would like to see me married again before they leave their bodies. Stories have stories within their stories, don't they?)

We parked and went in the large chain shoe store, our coupons ready. Sometimes just walking up and down the aisles for half an hour can clear the mind-sticky-ness. Every once in a while we found our size and tried on a shoe, or two. Mom picked out a nice pair of round-toed flats. I found nothing. She bought the shoes and we left. "In that whole store you couldn't find anything?" she sort of asked-said (wanting me to be happy). "No, nothing I really liked. No worries Mom, I had fun just looking." Our next stop was for ice-cold coffee-smoothies at a local place with a walk-up window. It was more like going to a local Dairy Queen, or Mr. Softy, and getting creamy-frozen coffee in a cup you could suck through a very wide straw, (when it comes to ice cream, soft is great).

"So what's new?" We sat in her white Mercury station wagon with the windows down and drank. I expected this from Mom. She always wanted to hear about my "interesting" life (even when I thought I had nothing *really* interesting to share. . .). "George got me a new mattress and it's awesome!" I reported. "Really? Why did he do that?" she questioned. "We're friends, and his dear friend is in the business." "Well that's awfully thoughtful of him," she added. "Mom, you have no idea!" I replied with enthusiasm. We talked about Kyle and Tim, and job prospects, the house, and about the training program

I was developing for kids—wanting to get it from its knees to walking, both financially and for the kids' sake (their parents' too).

"I think you should write a romance novel," she unpredictably encouraged. (Mom says what seems to be random stuff.) I think she encouraged me for the possibility of it "going gold", and all that money I'd haul in as a bestselling author, which might then save the house. Mom was about making money, and she knew I was having a wrestling match with that for longer than I had wanted. *"Oh sure Mom, I'll do that on Wednesday,"* I heard in my head. *What was* she thinking?! I can't write a romance novel! What the heck *is* a romance novel anyway!? Jackson-man never made it into the conversation. At least not then.

We drove to her house and walked inside. I said hello to Dad who was sitting in his usual chair at the dining room table writing, yet another book, (how funny that's where I sit and write in my house). I kissed them both, thanked Mom for shopping and the coffee, and left. It was Saturday afternoon and I wanted to get back to Nikki for a walk. I also had some client work I needed to complete and more job applications to send out.

On the way home around 2:00 p.m., I got a text from Jackson-the-man, (I didn't really need to tell you "the man" right?) I must have given him my number, I hadn't recalled. (Maybe he knew?) "What are you wearing ☺ wanna play later?" was all I could read at the stop light. His spirit was charmingly funny. Strange how something so nice can bring on fear too . . . *A second night out? How much later? Where did he live? Can I get everything done?* (Oh how the fragmented, fearful mind can roam!) I was driving so I didn't answer. I was home another ten minutes later.

Nikki greeted me eagerly as I closed the front door behind me. Tim was out again, and I had a few hours before it was Nikki's dinnertime – she's an early eater. I headed upstairs to change out of what I was wearing and back into my yoga pants and t-shirt. (Obviously it's my favorite home-wear.) Sidetracked, I started dusting my room. I dusted the shelf on which the gold can with Jackson's ashes sat. On top were all of his dog tags. His turquoise plaid Dog Whisperer collar (given to him), used to be there too. Now Nikki was wearing it. Her old one had gotten too small. I held the handful of tags, which offered vaccination and contact information, like a collection of charms connected to a single experience of love. I missed him deeply, again. There remained still, an intense yearning to hold him and look into his eyes to see that steady warmth and welcome. When imagining he was gone (from "here"), my eyes burned. I deposited the charms back on top of the can after dusting it, and remembered Nikki would be hungry soon, and I had

work to do . . . I wondered how love got so entangled
with fear? I think it happened when I forgot to notice the
entanglement. Once noticed, fear always seems to give
way, back to love, (not sure why . . . but I *had noticed
that*). I walked downstairs, noticing my fears connected
to Jackson-man, wanting to see every last one so they
would all dissolve and point me to love . . .

While I made Nikki's dinner, I sat my journal in front
of me and wrote down the fear about being in a
relationship with my dog, I mean my dog as a man. And
that's not actually accurate either. Jackson-man
described it better when he said, "*I seemed to have
'received', in this form, a good amount of Jackson-dog's
experience . . . Which is why I'm drawn to you. I have
other experiences too . . . and all of it blends.*" Did that
just happen for him seven months back when J-dog died?
Had he come from Mississippi with it? I had questions
. . and what the heck *is* reincarnation anyway!? I had
some research to do, and an overdue text to answer . . .

5

The Tub

"Sticky Notes are notes you refer to when you get stuck."
That's what Mom says. I've even thought of designing an
"app" (software application) that would offer new
considerations and wise information, whenever "stuck";
such as right now, when wanting to respond to a text
and fighting with myself, versus simply "flowing"
gracefully with the whole damn thing, by sending over
some amusing words . . . Why wasn't I cool, calm and
collected like those women in all those James Bond 007
movies who were my role models, when I was a kid!?
How were they always so perfectly, feminine-ly
confident?! I had watched them all! What hadn't I
learned?!

"Yes." I typed in the text box on my cell. Well, that was
confident . . . although five hours later. "7:30 p.m. pick
up?" came back like magic. *Did I ever tell him what I was
wearing?* . . . "Sure. What r we doing just want to make
sure I wear the right shoes ☺" I text back wanting to

know more. "going to the city...yes?" *Ooooo, yes, yes-yes!* That meant Manhattan. Seventy five minutes in, and oh the possibilities. "YES C U @ 7:30." I confirmed with the poise of a Bond Woman.

I had two and a half hours—an hour and a half to sit at the computer and get some things done, and almost one hour for Tub Time. By 6:30 p.m. there was a wanting to really look at those fears (so I could have a good time later, sort of get them out of the way). So I created a Sweat Lodge in the bathroom and proceeded to give myself permission to investigate. The fears were making me sick when I wanted to have fun, damn it.

Any misty bathroom can be the perfect Sweat Lodge . . .

> *Why such melancholy? . . . which sounds like cauliflower . . .* (crazy mind links, right?)

> *This feels so nice. This water . . . That guy . . .*

> *"When it's right, it doesn't have to take as long, as when it's wrong."* (My friend Leo's voice arose from the sweat.)

> *What does "right" mean anyway!?*

> *He never liked thunderstorms. He would crawl between my legs for assurance . . . yet . . .*

> *He plays trumpet, piano and drums . . . kind of a nice variety.* (Admiring the man was happening.)

All that stuff was noticed and captured first, in my Journal. The ink on the page had swollen from so much moisture in the air, and along with writing, it looked as if I had painted pictures around the words.

Sticky Notes, notes which to refer to when stuck . . . (an app?), ok, so what words of wisdom would unstuck the fear that keeps making me want to suck on ginger chews because of the nausea?" I asked myself rather logically, and then sank ever so slightly into the steamy-hot water. I held my pen and Journal high and jotted down everything that surfaced from everywhere . . .

> *It doesn't really matter what the thought, belief, interpretation, meaning IS. It only truly matters that you are aware of it . . . then laughing can begin . . .*

> *When aware of all that "matter-less information", like thoughts and ideas you are automatically in the field (or sandbox) of all possibilities. A great experience to feel. I think it's built-in to the whole-bloomin'-system.*

> *All thought is an experience. Which thoughts feel really good?!*

Self-counseling was happening. I had "picked up" stuff on my human antenna . . . (*from where does this s#!% arise?*) I put the Journal and pen on the floor hoping the ink wouldn't swell too much more. Then I began tapping. (Tapping is sort of a meditation; a focusing on a thought while tapping on parts of the skull, chest, hands, and such. All that tapping, focusing, noticing . . . and therein starts the smile. Cool practice.) I began to feel grateful, thankful even wealthy in that Sweat Tub Lodge. Jackson-dog's head appeared through the mist, and every molecule of water and air in that bathroom began to pulse with that warm, welcoming love, that came right through him. I swear it was like being, for a moment, in a silky soft pink womb, and *knowing* it. He looked right at me and "that look" was timeless, border-(Collie)-less, spacious. It *defined* the word "love". I knew that feeling "in my waters", as my dear friend Rhea would say. I knew it without words. (We all know it without language. It is the life-milk we are implanted with.) Last I hear . . . "*no blame, only love*". And I sighed with a crack of a smile. I left the Lodge more cleansed, more aware, than when I had entered. A renewed awareness felt wonderful, and I was going to *use it!*

What would I wear? It was 7:10 p.m. "Niiiikiii!" I called, once in the bedroom with still plenty of time to play. She came upstairs. "I am going to Manhattan with Jackson, man. I will leave the dog-door open, water, some lights on, and of course the bedroom door is open, and Nirvana would love your company . . . Help me figure out what to wear . . . " Nikki has the biggest smile when she's happy. All her teeth show, a bright white set of choppers with a bubble gum pink tongue in between. It is a remarkably rosy display. Jackson had a dark bluish tongue, which the Vet assured me was due to some "Chow in his mix". It was gorgeous too. I loved the experience of a spectrum of dog-tongue-colors. Somehow that always amused me.

Now I was ready to experience Jackson, (man/dog), tongue and all, with a new familiarity. Nikki and I quickly chose a short little button-down polyester dress, "50 shades of grey". A mod print. Yes, three-quarter sleeves, (love that look). I was inspired by polyester at the local consignment shops, (and for some odd reason it didn't attract dog fur like cotton, or knit). I took my silver dancing sandals with the low skinny heels, and stuck them in a shoe bag (just in case), then picked up my black pumps. Before slipping into them, I noticed my toes and shook my head as if to say, "No, no, no, this won't do", (there just didn't seem to be enough time to groom perfectly). I slapped some clear nail polish on every nail I owned, and walked around barefoot, waving my hands through the air till dry. Ok, that felt better. By then I was laughing. The seriousness of my entanglement with my fear was loosening! Playful was returning! Yaaaaaay! If there was anything this "Twilight Zone" experience was offering, (did I say "Twilight Zone", I didn't mean that, I meant "completely surprising romance"), was a rescrambling of my fearful, sad, angry "matter-less-ness" into meanings of love. (This supported me enormously, while trying to supply the bank with information that would cause them to want to work together on my continued home-ownership! The gripping fear that had had me in its story for two-plus years, which I'm certain added to my sleepless tossing and turning nights, was now lessening, relaxing, being replaced with new, life-affirming possibilities. How curious.) Nikki and I left the bedroom with fur flying, shoes and a light jacket jammed neatly in a bag. I was prepared for anything. (I even considered bringing sneakers . . . right . . . excessive.)

Again with Journal in hand, (yes, it's habitually glued to my hip), we scurried out to the back deck and garden, (my favorite room in the house), to create a few Sticky Notes from the stuff that had shown up during the Sweat Lodge. And, while sucking on yet another ginger chew, out popped the crown which had replaced one of my back, right molars. *You can't make this stuff up!* I couldn't believe it! *Now?! Now!? Really!?* I promptly wrapped it in tissue knowing I couldn't do anything with it till Monday, ran to the nearest mirror to check how "bad" it might look. Now I suddenly felt like an even *older* woman who was loosing her teeth, instead of a bright young, 40-something, sexy, single Mom, who was awaiting her dog-man-date. I wasn't smiling as widely, yet. I condensed and documented the tub illuminations,

1. *Awareness of my thoughts, the good, bad and ugly, causes laughing . . . eventually . . .*

2. *With awareness of my thoughts, more ideas show up. (I think it's built-in to being Human.)*

3. *Which ideas feel really good? Notice those!*

Yes, those were good Sticky Note additions to refer to. I wanted to get them to Mom by email in the morning.

Then I added #4,

> *Crown or no crown, (on tooth or elsewhere) . . . see only beauty!*

My internal dialogue was improving . . . and Jackson would arrive shortly.

6

100 Haunts

I stopped chewing on ginger chews and sucked them instead, since I now had one less tooth, (yet still beautiful, so I did not get crazy-nervous about that . . . I had known this "guy" for eight and a half years, right, sort of . . .?). It was 7:30 p.m. Nikki didn't bark, and Jackson was at the door once again on time. I *liked* that! I liked on-time-ness! (*An expectation is met when there is on-time-ness—how neat is that?!* I felt considered when there was on-time-ness!)

This time (no pun intended), with a more open heart and not so many preconceived-fears, I welcomed him in, in so many ways. Our eyes connected and that warm "love-look" was shared and acknowledged. I was beginning to notice this love-look experience in many ways, when transcribing my notes, just an hour before in the garden, every single plant, bird, bug, droplet of water, etc. seemed to look back at me with that look; that fundamental warmth and welcome inherent in all of what's here. It appeared through the mist in a pink-womb experience. It didn't just appear from one place, and not another. Jackson's love-look legacy was influencing me. I had begun to accept it could spring from everywhere, and where it wasn't, there might simply be entangled, limited, destructive matter-less-meaning bullshit, taking importance instead . . . *because it didn't know any better!!*

Tonight was going to be great fun. *I could feel it in my waters*, and nothing external had changed. It was an inside job, (bravo Sweat Tub Lodge)! I grabbed my "wardrobe" packed bag, left another note for Tim, and Nikki was in the big brown leather chair with access to the garden. Life was good.

Outside the air couldn't have been more delicious. A late May evening in the North East is a miracle. Back in his SUV, Jackson cued up Earth Wind and Fire, (another of my favorite 70's music sensations), and adjusted the volume perfectly. I was in heaven. I was sitting next to a sensually handsome man, with a melty-voice, who when looking into his eyes, I was transported to Divine Land, I was surrounded by beat, and, I was sitting up high! (Takes so little! lol) The conversation flew in a million directions with lots of laughter, what more was there to want at that moment?! (I was smiling wide with no "toothless-fear". He was to my left!)

"I took my kids to an amazing flea market today.
We had a picnic . . . they found some records and I
picked up those golf clubs in the back, circa 1930's!" He
nodded backward, excited. He knew Golf antiquity?!
Wow. He has kids?! Wow. How old?! "It was such a
beautiful day for that! Love the clubs!" I commented
with delight, (they were beautiful clubs, and I have this
belief that any divorced man who has experienced Dad-
hood, I share a connection with.) "How old are your
kids? Boys, Girls? You know Tim and Kyle", I amused.
He jumped right in, "19 and 24, two amazing young
women." Another wow! I liked the way he had said that.
It felt so authentic. *Maybe he could say anything and I
would be beguiled by that voice.* "Where do they live?"
I continued. "The 24 year old is in Manhattan and the 19
moves back and forth between her Mom's place and
mine." Wow. That sounded just like me . . . kind of. . .
Kyle was almost 24 and in Manhattan and Tim at 19 was
home with me. I was noticing my thinking again . . . *he
must drive into the city a few times monthly to be with
his daughter* . . . He switched CD's to Stevie Wonder's
newest. He shared whom he experienced his girls to be,
and I did the same, describing my sons. The ease and
comfort of the exchange felt lovely. I was enjoying "me"
in the "relationship" of "us"! That was most wonderfully
sweet. (I think when we like who we are in any
experience, it's the icing on the cake, as the "ego" is then
happy too! lol) Leo's phrase, "When it's right, it doesn't

take as long, as when it's wrong!" popped back into my awareness. (Love Leo's perspective! May add to Sticky Notes . . .) And so in the SUV it was going, instantaneously light, with the heaviness of "fear" and "wrong" absent (. . . I'm just sayin').

Through the tunnel and we were in the City. Yes, he knew his way. He must have had one hundred haunts he visited and revisited, in different moods, (with and without his daughters). Sometimes with the Trumpet, he would join whatever band was entertaining. Sometimes he would hop on a piano, electric or not, or set of drums (which he offered, were very much like playing piano . . . hmm, you pound on both?) He radiated when telling how he would, "roll with the sound . . . with the players". For him, music was a muse.

We were in midtown. Having left the SUV in the lot, I wore my silver dance shoes just in case, (they were as comfortable as slippers.) I stuck my lip stick, a ginger chew, and my cell in my jacket pocket, and left the bag. We walked to a nearby old-world restaurant with creaky worn wooden floors. We were lead outside to a trellis and seated under it, at a corner table dressed in white linen, set for two. I heard a faint echo in my mind, *"Did he plan this?"* I was pleasantly, surprisingly unconcerned with my toothless-ness. (Was it practicing all those Sticky Note perspectives?)

Here's the part where I want to make a few statements about the human body. First, most of us have not been trained (I wasn't) in feeling our body's orgasmic potential. In other words, trained in experiencing all of our "sensing" fully. So a good place to begin such training is with food, (and I'm not someone you would call a "Foodie"). All you need is just a little bit, in order to experience the very next thing your body does, (which is hopefully not an allergic reaction), the body is so perfectly, uniquely, fine tuned! So when the tart and sweet and rough and silky weave itself together on your tongue, in your mouth, even the insides of your cheeks enjoy what's happening (which sends signals to the rest of you)—it's an all-in-one connected experience. Also, if you happen to be with others, they too, feel the "sense-ually-orgasmic" experience you're having; as you do theirs, or not, of course, it's a potential "win-win" for all.

So yes, we did have the most amazing tapas and cocktails . . . every aspect of me was buzzing with joy (and not because of any alcohol . . . I am not a drinker . . . maybe an ice cold Corona on a hot afternoon, at most). My insides were having the time of their life with the pings and zaps of flavors and smells, not to mention I think he had on my favorite men's cologne . . . Need I say more? And joy like this expands, so to allow for the expansion to go to new heights, he knew right where to go to dance our fulfilling food and drink experience into the universe, in continued exaltation! So that's just what we did about eight blocks south . . . till the wee hours, (the lot where we left the SUV was 24/7).

The place was rockin'. There is just something about an awesome light show that syncs up with sound, and all those people with all that energy bouncing around smiling. You rarely see a frown, or scowl, on the face of someone dancing at a club! And, it had been such a long time since I had been in the city with a guy, and a very cool (or hot!) one at that. It was extraordinarily transporting (we humans have done this—danced ourselves into trance globally since we emerged here)! I had experienced two nights of Jackson, and three in Nirvana with Nikki. My "now" couldn't have been better . . . until . . . I saw something. It happened that fast. I can't even recall what it was that I saw, as I scanned the sea of humanity and observed their relationships. Yet, whatever it was I saw, or smelled, or heard, or felt in some way, it was just enough to trigger a thought so completely contrary from the fun I was having. What makes thoughts *do that*—change so fast?! What causes the linking in the mind so that one moment I'm immersed in the music, the man and the wave of human-rhythm-love, and the next I am sitting in a booth for two in dread, (Jackson-man had left for the men's room). Everything that "wasn't working" in my life, the way I wanted it to, arrived to haunt me—right there and then. Was I having way too much fun and so the "Guilt Patrol" came to assure there would be fear among joy? Was I having a panic attack?! Why?! Why now!? The mind is a terrible thing to waste with so much (screwy) fear! Once it gets filled up with that, next thing you know you're a goner down the slippery slope. First I was in paradise and then not. I was going fast, hearing every lousy conclusion. . . . *homeless, no money, no value . . . I let my sons down, what am I doing here, on earth, in this club . . . with this man-dog(?), when I needed to get a job . . . which hadn't happened in over 323 applications in more than two years . . .* which obviously *wasn't enough, and my kids program . . .* yadayadayada, and then the kicker emerged, *and I killed my dog!* (I certainly thought I had dissolved that one.) Why was this stuff intensifying when the potential for fun and happy was surrounding me?! Was I too scared of "good"!? Damn! Did I suffer joy always!? Crazy how I, (we humans) can soar and sink and soar and sink and – WHAT THE HECK!?

Jackson returned from the men's room and sensed my despair through my wobbly smile. "What-up? What's streaming through that brain?", he asked with humor as he sat down. In the past I wouldn't have been clear on how to answer. That night I was; 007 Bond Woman here I am . . . "I'm afraid," I said rather matter-of-factly, surprising myself. "Afraid?" he flashed back. Sitting in the

tiny booth for two, we could hear each other, and talk.
I was halfway thankful. If Jackson was my pooch
reincarnate, I just wanted to curl up with him and look at
him and be instantaneously reminded of the solidness of
love . . . and safety, and belonging. What happened
instead, on my side of the fence was more fear (Ugh),
and the party all around felt like it had left me out . . .
only I knew once again, it was an inside job. How could
I be sitting in one exciting situation and experiencing a
completely different one, one that felt so damn broken!?
I wondered how much detail I should share, how much
did he already know? It was just seven months ago I was
whispering my concerns in his ears as if he, Jackson-dog,
was an infinitely deep well into which I could say
everything (he knew English), and my words would
return as comfort and joy through that "love look". Did I
have that opportunity now? "I'm not sure what to share
with you," I spoke. "I've just been taken-over by some
worries and they're holding the rest of me hostage.
Apologies for not being present in this wonderful place",
and then it happened . . . why, how, I have no flippin'
idea. I cracked open and every single one of my deeply
debilitating fears came pouring out of my mouth
(unplanned), which was accompanied by uncontrollable
weeping. *What movie was I in!?* "I have so much
unsettled stuff in my life! I'm uncertain about my home,
my income (which of course I felt the worst about), my
roof leaks, my tooth fell out, and I just don't deserve your

company! I'm basically a no-where person, going no-
where fast!" (Actually I was going somewhere and it
wasn't pretty.) He was passing me napkins so I could
wipe up all the wetness streaming from every opening on
my head, (except for maybe my ears). "Anything else?" he
asked inviting more. I was feeling like I just put Mount
Olympus on the table and he wanted to know if there
was anything *more?!* That stopped me cold and I
abruptly laughed. I think it was because everything that
had poured forth from fear, that I had thought made me
ugly, unworthy and un-lovable didn't seem to do that for
him, and that was funny! He wasn't turned-off (in the
least) by my expression of such anxiety . . . and now
neither was I! (I was a wreck"! People don't like people
who are wrecks! . . . do they?!) Jackson felt so "together"
so "in charge", so on top of his authentic game, so
plugged into goodness! I, on the other hand, had just
fely so unlike those Bond Women; unsexy, un-sensual,
unattractive, (hadn't he noticed the gaping hole between
my teeth?!)

Something was shifting within me . . . "I have fears too."
he gently acknowledged. "Really?" I said further patting
myself dry. "Yes," he went on, "such as will you like me as
much, with them? Will you like me as much as I like
you?" Ok, more tears. I just wanted to grab him and hug
all of him tight. The mascara I had applied earlier had
left dark grey stains down my cheeks. I must have looked

like something out of a Halloween farce. He helped clear them away with one last napkin. Even with this spontaneous arrival of fright, even with my swollen eyes, even though I felt as if I should be thrown out, I was . . . liked . . . *by both of us!?* Was this my Jackson, who loved me unconditionally, always? Nothin' like a little love reflected back to set things straight . . . (within)!

How quickly things can look so different—storm blows in, storm blows out. How do we keep up with being human!? His words were like a Sticky Note for unstuckness, and when the DJ changed his tune and played a funk-sample version of "Take All of Me", (Seymour Simons and Gerald Marks, 1931), there in the booth, we lovingly looked at each other, aware of the lyrics, and left for the dance floor. And even though a little unsteady from my purge, I came back fully to joy in that sea of people, my fears taking a backseat once again— *Hallefuckinglujah!* As I mentioned, the mind is a terrible thing to waste to so much fear and sadness and yet, looking back, it had in fact, made the experience even sweeter.

A casual stroll to the parking lot revived me even more. My right arm linked through his left, which gave him my toothless side, which didn't make a bit of difference . . . We played Old School R&B all the way home and I did more seat-dancing. Then he says glancing at me with a shifty smile, "So a guy goes into a pub and sits down at the bar. The bowl of nuts sitting near him says, "Nice shirt." The guy flags down the bartender and says, "What's with the nuts?" "Oh them", the Bartender replies, "they're complimentary." He turned to watch the road, and again at me, giving me a most ridiculous, devotedly, syrupy look. Jackson-man was a hoot! He shared his different caricature-accents from Bugs Bunny to those crazy-friendly "Amigos" penguins in the animated movie Happy Feet (which I had watched several times, even without my boys).

On the porch he nosed my nose, licked my lips, gave me a warm deep hug and said "Good night". "Will you text me when you get home?" I asked, still not knowing how far a drive it was from my house to his. "Of course" he replied. How was it possible we hadn't kissed? No worries, I thought . . . what a great thing to anticipate! I went inside to greet Nikki who was waiting and wanted to know everything. Back in Nirvana we stayed up Girl-talking. Nikki was so enthralled—especially about the part where I broke-down, or broke-out, or was consumed by fear . . . (Why the heck is fear so interesting even to a non-human!?) A text came after twenty minutes. "Home." Nikki and I fell asleep deliciously exhausted.

7

The Ball

"*You can't make any money as a writer . . . unless your
book is a Bestseller,*" was my Dad's counsel to me years
back, (which I sort of understood and accepted as him
protecting me. His books were academic, and those
were rarely best-sellers. It saddened me . . . I loved to
write—everything except romance novels . . .) So when I
spent time writing, my tail went between my legs
ashamed I was not doing the *kind* of writing that might
earn me, (my sons and dog/s), an income (. . . social
media writing?) I would feel as if the very act that
brought joy, was wrong. *Holy s#!%* did that suck, big-
time. And my home was in jeopardy! *My home was in
jeopardy and I was writing!* It was Sunday morning and
I was firmly in the tub exhaling over this thought with
Journal and pen in my little wet hands once again. Did
the morning in the tub really have to start with this!? (I
had such a wonderful time last night!) I then heard
myself apologizing! *"I am soooo sorrryy - I am soooo
sorrryy - I can't do anything else, anything more, I can't*

think anything different! This is it! Yadayadayada . . . " I
felt my face scrunching and the volume in my head
increasing. *"And, I've done the Cinderella thing far too
long and now I want to go to the Ball! How do I get
there?!"* (What can I say about my mind when in the
tub?) It wasn't quite a Sweat Lodge, yet hot water is hot
water and I was feeling very "in it" . . . which is why I so
loved the tub. It seemed to be my place of "expression"
and, it seemed to drive me back to joy once through all
the gnarly stuff.

"What kind of Ball do you want to go to?" arose from the
waters—I swear. Was *that* my Fairy Godmother?!
I looked around the room searching. *"No struggle!"* I
said quickly, *"The No Struggle Ball!"* "No, wait, wait . . .
Joy, lots of joy, *the Joy Ball, and I arrive as the stunning
Lighthouse of Love!"* How was it possible, just as I
finished yelling silently while in the water, laughing
happened?! Wow! I loved that tub! Even with its
porcelain and tiled walls in desperate need of repair, it
"reset" all of me, every time. *"Yes, the Ball of
Unconditional Love! I want to know it, feel it, bring it
forth, shine it out . . . can I think about it some more?"*
Who did I think I was addressing?! The tub had that
trance-like, dance-like divine quality. . . just like writing.

Once out of the bathroom, momentarily "clean",
I picked up my hand-me-down copy of, *Cutting*

Through Spiritual Materialism, by Chögyam Trungpa,
(1971), Lisa had given me last year (when clearing and
then renting her house). I had recently read it, filling it
with underlines on almost every page, and torn paper
bookmarks indicating particular statements of interest,
(and some that Mom and I might include in future
Sticky Notes). It felt like an old treasure. In it Trungpa
describes that we are going "to fight all the time", our
"mind-dialogue" will that is, (my translation), and as long
as we are not "aware of" (my translation) that mind-
dialogue, we could miss the "primordial space" (his
translation), and would forever *only be experiencing* a
very small aspect of what we *could* be experiencing,
while here, (seriously limiting my "dog-man" possibility
to something very scary and small). If the "primordial
space" isn't on your radar, seems you're screwed! Which
leads right into a very short look at reincarnation and
how learning a smidge about it, allowed for an even
greater welcoming of "J-man" into my life. Please know,
I think "the primordial space" Trungpa speaks of is the
space where I found, (find), myself when looking into
Jackson's eyes, either pair (dog, or man). Also please
know the Sticky Note additions I had compiled the
night before, I did send to Mom. Our reference list for
getting "unstuck" was growing nicely. It was gold,
toward having a better internal "mind-dialogue" and an
"external-life" (and certainly of me accepting, that just
when I think it's "the end", it isn't, it is . . . yes, yes, more

of a beginning . . . of something unexpected, and just right . . . and sort of the same . . . reincarnation?)

Sitting at the dining room table with Nikki tucked neatly at my feet again, (she, I think, was getting used to me and the space there, without Jackson), I Googled "reincarnation". A fountain of information poured forth— posts to video—expressing the possibilities of life, after life, after life. I learned that there are two parts to the word originating from Latin, of course, (from where all English words seem to have been forged). "Re" meaning "back again" and "incarnate" meaning, "made flesh". Put the two together and you've got, "back in the flesh again"! (Oh the things we humans construct!) When connecting this, with some of the newest scientific findings which report "we are, *everything here is*" made of "energy" and "energy" doesn't "die" or "leave" or "dissolve" it simply changes *pulse*, (I know, a lot of quoted words), reincarnation seemed more "real", more possible. I also learned that in Indian religions, belief in a return of a "soul or spirit into a new form", is accepted as "business as usual". What else did I need to know, or did I simply require this information to process over time (. . . maybe in a future tub session)?

Reincarnation or not, the next time I saw Jackson-man my plan was to kiss . . . enough of being nosed and licked! I was hoping kissing would happen soon (*was that asking too much . . . even though we had known each other for eight and a half years!?*)! What did *he do* for a living? How long was *he* married? Does he like his Ex? . . . Maybe her name is Nikki! (lol)

I didn't hear from him that Sunday. I imagined he might be with his girls . . .

8

Reflection

Almost one year to the day, wonderful "Trundle-bed-Lisa" returned from California, this time to sell her house (within a month!), and not just rent it. This time everything inside and out, had to go. We met Monday early afternoon, at the same café where I had met Jackson almost one week earlier, to brainstorm the logistics of holding a major—immediate—yard sale; more like an estate sale. Lisa's taste in stuff was impeccable, so the remaining contents of her house was worth thousands and she invited me to split the take. She needed help. At least $3,000 for both, was a figure that seemed reasonable in such a short time-frame. And that chunk of change would help us enormously. I had treated the sale as if she were a new client. I was very serious about the details and, we had lots of catching up to do and oh how we did it! Our conversations were always layered and this one was no different. "Lisa, I can feel it in my waters, you're going to sell the house for twenty thousand more than you're asking! You may even have a bidding war!" I said that absolutely sure of myself, for no reason at all, (other than that's what had shown up for me). "Really!?" she perked up at the thought, her monetary fear, momentarily gone. "I'll take the first buyer who meets my price!" she quipped wishing for just *one* buyer, (while imagining that *that* might not even happen). We lost track of what we were saying several times, yet continued seamlessly until she asked about the trundle bed. Hmmm. "It's in my basement" I offered sheepishly. "In your basement! What, why!?" was her unhappy reply. "Lisa, that conversation will keep us here till closing. I love the trundle and will use it again, someday." I was quietly envisioning the whole comical mattress saga. What I wanted to tell her about was Jackson-the-man of course. I hadn't shared it with anyone, but we had so much planning to do and so little time, (was my internal chatter, followed by a loud and clearly unanimous internal *"So what!? Time, Bah, Humbug!"* "Lisa?" From the tone of my voice she knew I had opened a new matter. "What do you know about reincarnation?" "Reincarnation?" she reflected back with a slight tilt of her head. The night Jackson had left his dog-body, I was on the phone with Lisa. "Do you believe it's possible?" I pushed, " . . . that it can occur?" "Well first of all, *everything is real*, isn't it? We feel our nightmares intensely *real*. Right?" Did I mention Lisa was a Gestalt therapist, (certified by the best), had a great practice till she retired two years ago, rented her house, and next thing you know she's lovin' southern California, and not even 50 yet, (plus, she had "divorced well financially" and there is something to be said for that, something I had not done . . . (another story). She went on, "So let's put aside the word real and just look at the possibility of 'the same energy' showing up somewhere else . . . " She was deep into the question following the red thread, "You know scientists agree that *everything* which exists is made up of teeny, tiny sub-atomic particles we can't even see, right? Picture it? Snow-globe like . . . after you shake it, it sparkles and shimmers and moves. And when all that stuff or those particles, move and interact, they sort of "*see each other*," bounce, or reflect themselves *off-of*, or *on-to*, each other. I think it's all *that crashing interaction* actually, that *is light happening*; sun to star to light bulb . . . to idea," (she always had a unique perspective). I think that *is reflection* happening . . . the moving-dynamic of a bunch of tiny stuff all balled up, *lighting up* at the 'sight of each other' . . . at the 'speed of light'!" We locked eyes and broke out smiling. "Everything—matter and the matter-less—is always moving and reliant on each other, in order to exist," she sang out, "so reincarnation and existence might then seem more like *reflective* experiences." "Go on," I invited her at the edge of my café chair, not yet clear on how I was involved in Jackson's reincarnation into human form, "*guilt by reflection*"? "Well," she seriously continued, "for the human experience what reflects—bounces back—seems to be

according to *what's* looking! Are you following?" She
gazed her green eyes into mine, effectively keeping me in
her positive trance. "Imagine it this way, imagine it's not
the mirror that's important, yet rather the *translation of
what's seen in the mirror* that makes every experience!
We both may be surprised by the same event—same
bounce—yet our response to it, the intensities we feel
about it will be quite different." I was more than half-
getting what she was saying, my eyes urged her onward,
"So if *what's translating*—the you—let's say is missing
Jackson terribly, and energy has a reflective quality,
wouldn't those thoughts of missing Jackson, or some
aspect of them bounce back eventually? Or never? At
least two possibilities could co-exist, and so one day you
look up and Jackson is, has, 'reincarnated' back in front of
your face . . . although differently!" *Was she psychic too!?*
She added, "Reincarnation might be a new, blow-your-
mind, highly useful experience." *(Yup, the human brain is
like no other we know so far . . . pretty, pretty impressive
. . . (lol).* She went on, "Sure seems reasonable to me. In
wisdom traditions it's 'spirit returning', may as well be
'reflection happening'," she summarized theologically,
culturally and scientifically, " . . . . we are either aware of
it, or not. *You* happened to want to be aware of it!" It
was all music to my (reincarnated?) ears!

She had spoken my language, the one of possibility
versus "no way". Then out of my mouth rolled

(I think because I felt an invitation, an opening to explore), "Well, hmmm, (pause) now that you've mentioned it . . . would you believe that just last week in this very café, a guy came up to me and introduced himself as *Jackson* . . . and, I don't mean some *random Jackson* fellow . . . he actually said he was *Jackson-dog*." I looked directly at her for some new signal that I wasn't losing my mind, nor already delusional from life-concerns. "Lisa, he has the same eyes, or actually the same *loving-look* as Jackson!" I added. A great silence from a frozen stare of disbelief was not the most pleasant response . . . nor was it what I wanted. When her thaw would happen was way too suspenseful. "Lisa! Breathe. Please!" I grunted. "You're kidding, right?!" she coughed out grinning "No I'm not." I said, rather serious and continued, "You think I would joke about this? She interjected with a "Yes". (Ugh.) "I suppose that might make a rather interesting tale, yet no. We've been on two dates," I shared. "Really? Is he anything like J-dog?" she inquired calmly and went on asking another question, "What does Nikki sense?" "Good question! She knows him," I said, " . . . it's startling how much . . . and he's so handsome," I grinned wide, like the Cheshire Cat in Lewis Carroll's *Alice's Adventures in Wonderland.* "Well," she flipped back chuckling, "he *was a handsome dog!"* Again, another laughter outbreak! It was getting late. I filled her in on the dancing, the licking, and his rather early suggestion to live together! (Did I really

know him? I couldn't possibly *know the man* . . . all that
blended with the J-dog spirit, knowledge, wisdom, and
habits. Jackson-dog hated thunderstorms and fire works.
Loud explosions caused him to wedge himself between
my legs, (Tim had always laughed at that). In his SUV,
on one of our dates, Jackson-man informed me he *loved*
all that banging and booming from thunder and
celebrations . . . was that connected to his love of
percussion; drumming, banging on the piano, horn
blowing? Yet, *what I did really know about him*, was
that love-look. I knew that deeply. "Can I meet him
before I fly back home, I'll vet him and make sure he's not
some psycho!" Lisa jousted and I responded, "Maybe *I'm
the psycho* missing my dog and then manifesting a new
man-dog-reflection!?" I was half serious and continued,
"Yes, of course you can meet him." To Lisa the whole
thing was a amusing . . . she was so very supportive. We
stayed another hour drafting the "Estate Sale To Do
List" then we walked to her house, and I walked another
three blocks home.

I fed Nikki and thought of George, who was back in
Florida on business. What the heck might he say about
my new man-friend? I emailed Vince a more buttoned up
version of the bed-testimonial I had texted to George,
"The mattress is heaven. I now go to bed smiling and I
wake up smiling! I've named it Nirvana!" was something
he could post on his website. "I have the best fucking

bed", was not.

Sinking into Nirvana at about 10:00 p.m., the man with the love-look called. I must say that being *in* Nirvana and hearing a voice like his was, well, better than hot bread with sweet butter (one of my favorite things). "Hey there . . . how was your day, and would you like to join me Thursday evening for dinner?" Yes, yes, YES! That was going to be the night we would kiss . . . (if you don't *kiss well together*, how is it possible stay connected as partners . . . how do you move in with someone?!) *Do I have a limited view, or good instincts?!* Kissing is intimate, and I wanted to feel what it would be like with him (it had been so darn long since I had been inspired to kiss any man). And a blissful kiss feels as though you're fully in the same space-time-reality with your partner, or not! And if you're not, could a connection last . . . *(for me)*? Dinner was scheduled. I *had to have the crown put back in my mouth* securely between now and then. Don't you just hate the real-ness of fear?! (and sometimes there seems to be a fine line between the excitement of fear and the excitement of bliss . . . *right*?!)

John Tarrant is one of my favorite authors. Here is one reason why, "*It can be consoling to discover that you don't have to believe in your own thoughts.*" (Bring Me the Rhinoceros, p. 131) Relieving, isn't it? What a great uplifting notion! That was way better than any of mine! Here's another tidbit from the same book, "*What you can*

*conceive of might take away your life. On the other hand,
what you cannot conceive of might give you your life and
even unexpected joy."* (p. 53) Stuff like that is precious
toward establishing a great existence. So after having
meditated on that, when I phoned the Dentist office that
Tuesday morning around 9:00 a.m. with hot coffee on
deck with Nikki, (and another night in Nirvana), I had
lost the intense yearning that my crown *had to be put
back* before Thursday night. Go figure. It was more like
a smiling-smirk of pleasantness that there might be a
chance opening in the schedule on such short notice, and
guess what? "Bingo!" There was, "one availability" and it
was on Thursday afternoon! Life was already happening
with far less fear (and sadness) rearing it's ugly head, (. . .
and he already knew me without my tooth)! Other
people's perspective can be so reassuring.

At 9:48 a.m. and all smiles, the bank phoned. Why God,
why!? I knew their number and it still caused me to
shutter when it appeared on my cell, even though I was
quite familiar with the two people who were my "new
Contacts" and the only ones ever to call. Double ugh, ok
just one ugh really. It had been over two years of this
messy situation (did I say that), the length of time
extended from last year because my previous mortgage
holder was bought by a mega-bank back then, which
started the foreclosure process from the beginning. Then
I had a Lawyer, this time I didn't. And, even though my

"new Contacts" and I had spoken routinely for at least
six, or eight months, they still conducted themselves as if
we had met for the first time, every call . . . "This call is
being recorded for quality assurance yadayada." After the
consistent intro-disclosure, Terri spoke, "Hi, how are
you doing today?" My response was a pattern. With my
heart in my throat and my head in my stomach, I could
only ever express, queasy and half-smiling, "Pretty good
Terri, thanks, and you?" They had a tomb of data on me;
bank statements, taxes, quarterly Profit & Loss
statements. I had been in a heightened prickly limbo,
pending a decision, for way too long. Then Terri went
on, "We would like to invest in you, and have structured
a few plans we think will work well over time, for both of
us." *WHAAAAT!? Was she kidding?!* Winning a billion
dollar lottery couldn't have felt any more dreamlike, or
divine! The bank wanted to work with me—invest *in me!*
Was I really hearing that, accurately, in "real time"? *This
was New Jersey!* I had just booked a perfectly timed
dentist appointment and now this!? "*Depend on the
inconceivable*", John Tarrant spoke to me, and even
though I had dreamed about this possibility happening
in "real life, real time", until the damn thing actually
manifested, doubt would prevail taking down the
sinking ship over and over, every time. Not now! This
call was a miracle! "Terri, I am so delighted to hear this!"
I showed some composure, when I just wanted to fling
the phone into the air and run out the front door and

down the street in joy shouting, "They want to *WORK* with *ME*, they have a *plan*, a *structure* that might *work well over time!*" I held on to the phone with my sweaty left hand, while taking detailed notes on what she was describing with my right. "I will send all this to you in an email and contact you next week, " she concluded. Ok, good, I didn't need to be so concerned with my notes. "That should give you plenty of time to review," she finalized and with a few more yadayada's, I replied. "Perfect Terri, I'll confirm I received it. Looking forward to next week." We hung up. Holy, holy, *holy* synchronization Batman (. . . maybe you have to be older than 50 to get that reference?)! I poured another cup of coffee, plunked a few ice cubes in this time and smiled big at Nikki. The fear of loosing my home, in an instant, now had no meaning, or purpose. POOF. How quickly things can change, (. . . really!? Quickly? It had been over two years)! I felt like Dorothy in The Wizard of Oz, having never achieved "going home" and then, BAM! Home. I landed unexpectedly! It was time to call Mom and Dad, and Tim and Kyle, and share the inconceivable (yet imagined)! It was a most remarkable morning.

Within what could appear, as a short duration of time (two months, two years?), I had received a new bed, had met my dog wearing a human coat, my teeth were scheduled to be cleaned and repaired, and now I had confirmation that my house would remain my home, even with the little income that was in-coming! Had I "reflected it" to happen all along and not even noticed? Had I just *thought* I wasn't doing "enough", and I was "doing just fine" on the "execution" of everything; keeping the lights on, the kid-program going, writing assignments, job prospects, Mom-hood, daughter-hood, and friend-hood to some, and now becoming aware of the love-look? (Jackson's life and death was becoming just fine too.) Was everything happening perfectly on time (I LOVE ON-TIME!)

I sat at my computer and executed several hours of social media writing for two clients. Thursday my crown would once again fill the empty gap in my mouth and then I would kiss, not be licked, or nuzzled, by Jackson the man (*the handsome dog of my dreams?!*) . . . and after that, well, I hadn't reflected it yet. I just knew Lisa's Estate Sale would be profitable, (that's the way I wanted *that* reflected), and relying on the inconceivable was happening more often . . . Maybe we would do even better!

Yes I was drawn to polyester. It always looked new and the patterns and colors were very Emilio-Pucci-mod . . . fur didn't stick to it, and every time I wore that one particular "50 shades of grey" dress (yes that one), it was sure to "reflect back" a compliment from someone (for

some reason . . . maybe because I was so happy in it?).
Maybe when I attend the *Unconditional Ball of Love*,
I'll wear something polyester-slinky just like it. I
imagined Polyester wouldn't be around much longer
and, due to that, how sports clothes would change in
the future (yup, polyester is made from oil!) I was
considering my "Ball" outfit (and it's oily nature), as a
kind of mind-signal to myself that manifesting the Ball
experience, was definitely in process. Reflections were
happening the way I wanted, not the way I had feared
(*I was on the way to the Ball now!*)

Late that Tuesday afternoon, and a bit cooler outside,
was a perfect time for a woods-walk with Nikki. I suited
her up and we were one step closer to Happy Hour. She
hopped into the Jeep, on top of the back seat, which had
been folded-forward, with a white cotton blanket placed
on top just for her. There was magic in the woods in a
late May afternoon. Maybe it was all that good stuff
reflecting there, just waiting for us to walk among it and
bounce it back!? If something showed up on my radar,
(in my mind), now, I considered it a possible "reflection"
(of important information). "Go to the woods" had,
"shown up" and we were goin'. (As if the words were
simply translating my body's—already in motion—
direction. "All of me" had been taking care of me, more
than I had been aware of (all that crying a kind of
nurturing too). Which is why I now have great respect

and humility for "my equipment", my whole body-
meaning-making-system and how it keeps me alive
during freaky experiences; how I don't lift a finger and it
self-regulates! Which is exactly what it did when we met
Jackson off leash, in the woods, along with his very male
master, an Indiana-Jonesy-type-male . . . Really.

Both Jonesy and his dog had the love-look, or rather
reflected it, I felt, right there in the woods with the early
evening sun pulsing its honey-golden rays between the
spaces. I was feelin' the love beaming, as all four of us
came together (. . . was this another hallucination . . .
coffee had been way earlier . . .), the pups were obviously
happy. First words out of Mr. Jonesy's mouth were,
"Hi this is Jackson, and I'm Jones." He held his hand out
for a shake (the man) and I was thinkin', *No waaaay! No
way! Jackson? Jonesy? Had he read my mind too?!
Can everyone read my mind,* or was it the reflection of
my mind bouncing back, telling me what was there?!
(OMG!) I looked around as if to rule out a camera crew.
Does he know who I am!? *I'm* Jackson's Mom! Again I
probably looked stupid with my jaw hanging down a bit
in the shock of the inconceivable. My saving grace was
the recovery time. Accepting what was happening
quickly was useful, after the initial recoil. Was it the
name Jackson . . . Jonesy? Were the names signaling me
to "Attention" and then validating where the love-look
was, where it could be experienced, where it lived, how it

feels, (now that "his eyes" weren't here like they were, to offer it)? Was it the universe training me, educating me to know the love-look was ever-present? *"Haha! Hey You! Your dog Jackson—the-love-walking-dog—is over there and there, and here, and over there too, through that dog and that man, and that tree, and that bird, and that star and moon, and oh yeah your Mom and Dad too, and always your boys . . .* If it's here in this "reality", it has to have the potential to offer the love-look and, I, to reflect it back! (Another Sticky Note?) What the heck was going on *now*!? (I thought about what I had for breakfast.) The four of us stood there in a bubble of benevolence, I sharing, "I had a Jackson too . . . " I looked into their eyes, my gaze naturally alternating. Speechless, a little teary, and plenty "said". When we parted ways, Nikki licked Jackson on the nose, and Jonesy, who was actually a theoretical physicist (no kidding), left me with one thing to consider, "You may be interested in getting to know the term, quantum entanglement." Wow! Was he too pointing to, and educating me on, reincarnation, or reflection, from his scientific perspective? I thanked him and made a mental note. The woods had offered the love-look, reflection and entanglement . . . were they *all* the same?

I pulled the Jeep up to the house and Nikki began happy-barking. There on the porch were the most beautiful purple, blue and goldy-orange tulips, peonies

and hydrangea in a delicately tall crystal vase. Who?
What? The inconceivable was bouncing all over . . . my
favorite flowers! I parked, escorted Nikki up the steps
and she showed me where the card was secured. "How
sweeeet!" exclaimed my inner-voice as I read the hand-
written note. (Was this *his* handwriting—all CAPS—
I write like that too?!) Jackson was looking forward to
meeting again on Thursday, and yes, it might involve
dancing so "PACK YOUR GLASS SLIPPERS" (I
met a guy who loves to dance! Yaaaay!) That was so fun
to read! I wiped the mud from Nikki's paws and
underbelly with a car-towel, left my boots on the porch,
got us in the house, and went back for the flowers. I
placed them on the kitchen counter . . . flowers bring life
to everything.

What a Tuesday it had been. Nothing like it I can recall.
I had one (or two) more call(s) to make, as the evening
moved into night.

"Hi mom, guess what? The bank wants to work with
me! They called this morning!" "Wow! That is the best
news yet!" she replied thrilled. "I'll tell Dad!" We high-
fived over the phone and let out the biggest screams
of joy under the circumstances (very close neighbors).
I figured there was a worthy Sticky Note in the
experience somewhere. I would wait for it to show up . . .
I sent a group-text to Tim and Kyle and let them know
the bank had "structured a few good plans". The echoes

of "happy" were felt from many directions. (Could the love-look have sound?) I called George and Lisa, since they had traveled my insecure-homeownership-journey with me. George couldn't get over it, how unlikely it was for a bank (*especially in Jersey*), to decide to *work* with the homeowner! From Lisa, there was delight in knowing we were going to continue to be safe at home.

That night I went to sleep deeply again, Nirvana remembering just how to hold me. Wednesday morning the love-look was in Nikki's eyes. I hadn't seen it there, quite like that, before that moment, (ok, ok, was it me bouncing it to her . . . was it J-dog's influence)!? Maybe in all the bizarre-ness, I had *really been encouraged to beam the love-look* rather than only receive it. With this new thought, I was excited to see Jackson man.

I could hardly make it through Wednesday . . . which is why I think we should skip it, and go directly to Thursday and the anticipated kiss . . . somehow I was sure the love would be there. Please know, I did make one important call back to Mom, this time having a conversation about the man I had met at the café . . . and how he introduced himself . . . "*He might teach you something new!*" She exclaimed. "*You might eat the same foods, you might invent new things together!*" Mom's excitement got me excited (excitement is contagious). "*As your dog, he may have everything you want in a man!"* She thought that was funny. (Ok, I had been "without man" for a while.) *"Maybe he thinks you'd be a great person to be with, as a person, experiencing you now, at eye level!"* She was so pro check-him-out-further. I assured her I had planned on it, and would keep her informed, (I think we all live vicariously through each other, trying on dreams, or is that really just reflection too?) Go Mom! She also assured me Dad was in support . . . (How wacky was that!)

9

Perfect

Thursday morning Lisa and I met back at the café, for
further Estate Sale planning. We worked like a fine-
tuned system, filling in what the other left out. Yes, our
"take" would be even more than estimated, since she had
added a few new items she wasn't shipping west. The
new stuff would need to be researched for price. . . "So
you're going to ensure a kiss tonight?" She inquired like a
woman does, adding more spice to the conversation.
"Yup, that's my aim." I beamed back. "What if he doesn't
want to . . . isn't ready?" she posed. "Wouldn't every man
want to, we're talkin' *man* here?!" I gave a snarly smile.
"Really?" she replied looking at me with eyes narrowed,
"Maybe he's part something else! Ha!" The whole thing
was laughable and curiously kind of emotionally-serious.
I had to—wanted to—drop the seriousness. What was so
serious about meeting, (and kissing, not licking) a man
who had informed you he has some of your former dog-
partners traits, and knowledge and, wants to *be* with you
. . . Not so serious right!? . . .

My crown was put back in perfectly that afternoon. Having it back in made me aware of how much I had chewed on the left side of my mouth, for the week it was absent on the right, and how quickly I got used to something—good or otherwise—naturally adjusting, (hmmm, maybe Sticky Note worthy. . .).

As soon as I got home, I took Nikki, her dinner, and my journal out back to the garden, to write and regroup. It was a spectacular spring evening and I felt like taking a moment for reflection! (I was liking reflection.) Dinner and kissing wasn't for another three hours and my dancing slippers were always ready . . . and then, a Sticky Note clearly surfaced translating what was about to happen as I sat there with Nikki, and I hadn't a clue . . . "*Just when you think you have a handle on things, you may not, and that's good.*" Inconceivably, the very next moment after jotting that in the Journal on my lap, with my black felt-tip pen, I erupted in tears . . . about Jackson-dog. REALLY. Geez. (Just when you think . .) "*JACKSON!*" I cried upward to the evergreen bows creating the garden's canopy. "*COME BACK! FUCK!*" I MISS YOU SO! . . . "*COME BACK AND PLAY WITH ME! LOOK AT ME!*", slowly draining the story out into the air, sobbing, more sobbing . . . "*Love me the way you did! With that looook . . . COME*

BACK! SIT NEXT TO ME! KEEP COMPANY WITH ME!" In the seven months since I had "cancelled" his life, I thought I was done with such intense grief, (it was obviously a process). Staring at the garden's beauty, waterfalls flowing from my eyes, everything drenched (*again*) I bellowed, "COME BACK, COME BACK . . . *OR DON'T!"* (This was *way more* than regrouping.) COME BACK . . . *OR, OR DON'T!"* Or don't?! . . . and with those words, shot from no where, my crying ceased and a grin appeared, and I heard, *What if it's all perfect, what then?* What if *WHAT was perfect!?* I retorted aloud. *What if Jackson's death—how it went down—was perfect?* Perfect was now present as something crazy to consider (which hadn't ever happened before this). *Which would mean I hadn't "failed" what I had loved.* If it was all perfect, I had supported him, in all my not-knowing at the time—how about *that* story!? How extraordinarily odd life can be! At the apex of my cry I wanted Jackson back, and with the words, *"Or don't"*, a new, more loving, consideration appeared! (What a roller-coaster!) As if an energetic angry-sad-happy-orgasmic-story had burst through my form (like a gigantic sneeze) and now, I was happily aware of it. My psyche was the solution I had been bathing in, all this time. Somehow my perspective had shifted, and Jackson didn't have to come back—as he was. Nikki glanced over at me, as if, in agreement as I wiped myself (I think I used my shirt, would you believe

I'm really not a crier, yet with all that had occurred . . .
geez). The air was perfect, the garden was perfect and I
felt that ever-present love-look around me. Nothing
needed to be different to be good. And remarkably, a
Cardinal appeared on the Butterfly Weed bush, (how
randomly inconceivably perfect, they were rare in my
backyard). Upon seeing it I wanted a dress the color of
its feathers, I was so inspired (never owned a royal-red
dress)!

Not needing anything *different* from Jackson, or me,
caused me to consider with—great enthusiasm—flying
into a deeply human experience with Jackson-man!
Everything is sooo connected! (. . . I'm just sayin'.)

Something dank and heavy had fallen away, which
caused something wonderful to fill itself in (the love-look
was everywhere).

Another Sticky Note was in order, "Just when you think
it's the end, it's not." With renewed energy, I scooped up
my pen and Journal and Nikki followed me inside. I
wondered if my red eyes would return to normal by the
time my dinner-date (and if "the look" could be seen from
them, then whatever they looked like wouldn't hardly
matter). Nikki crawled into the big brown leather chair
in the living room. I excitedly set a hot tub as kissing-
prep (and put my journal away. lol). It was Tim's day off.
Maybe he was out with friends. He knew I would be out

for the evening (and maybe longer . . . *if the kissing was good*).

Without too much consideration of a beginning, middle or end of this story, I'd like to take you on a slight diversion . . . mostly because this story, the one you've been reading, is connected to an even larger story (yup) . . . and *that* story offers what I think, is an *even more remarkable* aspect to the *whole* story, if you can believe that. And, it happened in "real time".

10

"Real Time"

At the same time I, (the author, who really had a dog
named Jackson), was drafting "Jackson's Love", I posted
a "profile" on one of the online dating sites. My Mom and
Dad had bought me a three-month subscription—it was
on sale with a coupon, (coupons are useful for more than
just shoes). One night while writing yet another chapter
of what I thought to be a wild tale of fun, fear and
romance, (single Mom, two sons, two dogs . . . yadayada
—because Mom had challenged me to write it—yes),
I received an email that stunned me. Now, this was *"real
time"*, not "pretend" . . . although I'm no longer sure of
the distinction. The highly remarkable aspect of this
"stunning" online dating email was the very short essay
the man included in his note to me, and yes, his "profile
photos" showed he had big brown eyes. His look drew
me in. (*You can't make this stuff up!?*) One of the
sentences in his essay, which I read several times, that
sent chills echoing through me was, "*Remember I told
you about that house where I saw the 'reflection' of my*

dog Jackson?" Ok, reading that, yeah, stopped me cold (though I wasn't laughing). So did this, "*The house had wood floors and Jackson was a black lab with long nails, and whenever he walked inside his nails would tap on the floor.*" (Well so did my Jackson's nails!) *Who is this guy?! Had he read my mind toooo —can every one?! Am I soooo transparent . . . ?! I had just written about that!* I was frozen staring at the words. How were both experiences happening simultaneously?! I thought I was writing a fiction story, not actually experiencing Jackson's reflection, his spirit, in "real-time"! What *is* "real-time" anyway and *where the heck is it*, as opposed to "un-real time"!? Or "*pretend*"?! Of course, I responded to him . . .

The following day I received a "Hello," from yet another man with brown eyes. This one sharing that in his previous relationship they had a black Poodle named Jackson which "he got possession of in the breakup" and that, "Jackson and he, would be cool with any pet you might bring . . . " etc. Really! (*Have I mentioned you can't make this stuff up?!*) I was beginning to feel as if one aspect of me was living in one story, while another aspect was in a similar one, in some other "reality"! Fascinating! I replied to him too . . .

Is it really possible we are writing (speaking, thinking) our experiences into existence every second, and that this universe is so very "reflective" in its nature, with such strong "bounce-factor", that an occurrence such as Déjà vu, (French for "already seen") is more common place than originally thought?

When the men who wrote those notes faded into the ether, (*did I do that . . . ?*), I considered those "dating-connections" to be simple little reflections from Jackson-dog, bouncing over to me, insisting I stay the course and share this adventure, insisting that the love-look could be everywhere and known by everyone . . . insisting he is everywhere too—showing me what a love portal looks like. I didn't need Jackson back in his dog-coat. The night I released him into the cosmos played more "perfectly" in my mind—and the *reflections* didn't end there (just when you think . . .).

Guess what else happened while writing this story? Yesterday, a very new "Contact" from the bank, called. The young man and I struck up a rapport right away and during the exchange he actually spoke the words, "*I want to work with you, to get you a mortgage modification.*" He also said there was "no guarantee", yet, these days, seems I only need to *imagine* a "guarantee" and it would *reflect itself back in "real time"* (. . . I'm just sayin').

And John Tarrant rescued me again with more words from his book, "*It's nice to have your mind blown by a new concept, and dazzling ones are more fun.*" (p. 56!)

"YES I want to experience the Ball of Unconditional Love, I want to know it, feel it, bring it forth, shine it out, see Jackson's love-look in another's eyes . . ."

In the *throws of that*, Mom called and told me to go for a walk with Nikki and finish writing later.

As for Thursday night with Jackson (man!) . . . *how much time do you have?! Oh My Gawd! . . .*

Sticky Notes

"Sticky Notes are notes you refer to when you get stuck."
Just in case . . . eight notes for now . . .

1. Awareness of my thoughts, the good, bad and ugly, causes laughing . . . eventually . . .
2. With awareness of my thoughts, more ideas show up. (It's built-in.)
3. What ideas feel really good? Notice those!
4. Crown or no crown, (on tooth, or elsewhere) . . . see only beauty!
5. "When it's right it doesn't have to take as long, as when it's wrong!" (Leo's phrase)
6. Just when you think you have a handle on things, you may not, and that's good.
7. Just when you think it's the end, it isn't . . . (It's most likely a beginning.)
8. "Pretend", "Real", hmmm . . .

Dana Lichtstrahl

Mother, daughter, sister, aunt, niece, cousin, dog-
companion, friend, colleague . . . partner, lover, is a
"closet writer" (just coming out) who has also published,
Are You Watching . . . it's positively life-changing (non-
fiction, she thinks), and *not-so-fable FABLES* (definitely
fiction . . . kind of). You may contact her through,
www.danalichtstrahl.com.

www.ingramcontent.com/pod-product-compliance
Lightning Source LLC
Chambersburg PA
CBHW071127130626
46555CB00013B/1050